THIS IS ME!

INNER REFLECTIONS

Edited By Andrew Porter

First published in Great Britain in 2022 by:

YoungWriters® Est. 1991

Young Writers
Remus House
Coltsfoot Drive
Peterborough
PE2 9BF
Telephone: 01733 890066
Website: www.youngwriters.co.uk

All Rights Reserved
Book Design by Ashley Janson
© Copyright Contributors 2021
Softback ISBN 978-1-80015-770-5

Printed and bound in the UK by BookPrintingUK
Website: www.bookprintinguk.com
YB0493D

FOREWORD

For Young Writers' latest competition This Is Me, we asked primary school pupils to look inside themselves, to think about what makes them unique, and then write a poem about it! They rose to the challenge magnificently and the result is this fantastic collection of poems in a variety of poetic styles.

Here at Young Writers our aim is to encourage creativity in children and to inspire a love of the written word, so it's great to get such an amazing response, with some absolutely fantastic poems. It's important for children to focus on and celebrate themselves and this competition allowed them to write freely and honestly, celebrating what makes them great, expressing their hopes and fears, or simply writing about their favourite things. This Is Me gave them the power of words. The result is a collection of inspirational and moving poems that also showcase their creativity and writing ability.

I'd like to congratulate all the young poets in this anthology, I hope this inspires them to continue with their creative writing.

CONTENTS

Annanhill Primary School, Kilmarnock

Nathan Todd (9)	1
Kaden Wright (9)	2
Ailsa Wightman (8)	3
Beth Sommerville (9)	4
Devyn Alexander (9)	5
Millie Lindsay (9)	6
Bronte Harper (9)	7
Ruby Ferrara (9)	8
Jessica MacLean (9)	9
Jack Speirs (9)	10
Caitlin Hattie (9)	11
Daniel McGonigall (9)	12
Niamh Cunningham (9)	13
Finley McPike (9)	14
Jasmine Moore (9)	15
Lyle Anderson (9)	16
Ben Havlin (9)	17
Riley Reid (8)	18
Aric Alexander (9)	19
Ava Sword (8)	20
Elspeth Clelland (9)	21

Antrim Primary School, Antrim

Carson Magee (7)	22
Blake Lowe (7)	23
Sofia Jennings-Patrick (8)	24
Evie Murdough (7)	25
Zack McManus (7)	26
Audrey Robinson-Bradbury (7)	27
Lucas Fox (7)	28
Sienna Smyth (7)	29
Harrison Shaw (7)	30

Abbie Park (7)	31
Jithendra Appapantula (7)	32
Zixi Guo (7)	33
Carter Rogers (8)	34
Ana Burrows (7)	35
Poppy Stewart (7)	36

Horwich Parish CE Primary School, Horwich

Max Knight (8)	37
Leah Stokes (10)	38
Freya Rushworth (9)	40
Stephanie McCarthy (11)	41
Amelia Krinks (9)	42
Maya Ghosh (9)	43
Nathan Barrow (10)	44
Lucas Trow (10)	45
Frankie Topham (11)	46
Grayce Bulger (11)	47
Isabella Leach (10)	48
Toby Zarins (10)	49
Jacob Walton (10)	50
Mbali Ndlovu (10)	51
Isabella Benson (8)	52
Alice Cheetham (7)	53
Harrison Crossley (11)	54
Tia-Raani Tuplin (9)	55
Ella Bolton (7)	56
Eloise Marland (7)	57
Ben Slater (10)	58
Libby Fisher (7)	59
Jabe Cayton (11)	60
Ernie Mollitt (9)	61
Jorgie-Leigh Burrows (9)	62
Jessica Hope (9)	63

Daniella Burns-Camus (10)	64
Kaitlin Chapman (9)	65
Stanley Birbeck (8)	66
Niamh Wilkieson (9)	67
Jeffrey Smith (8)	68
Fern O'Brien (11)	69
Isabel Cheetham (7)	70
Amy Rose Grundy (9)	71
Everlie Williams-Hall (7)	72
Leila Tucker (10)	73
Olivia Gagg (7)	74
Layla Jackson (5)	75
Daniel Tonu (5)	76
Isabella Daley (6)	77

Scargill Junior School, Rainham

Olivia Gladden (10)	78
Ayaat Salawe (11)	81
Sade Majoyeogbe (9)	82
Libby Jobson (8)	84
Hannah Onaboye (8)	86
Tameem Wahhaj (10)	87
Hollie Morphew (10)	88
Zara Kasule (9)	90
Ana Maria Astefaniei (11)	92
Laiba Faheem (10)	93
James Fogg (7)	94
Lara Mahrous (9)	95
Chloe Summers (10)	96
Syed Azeem (9)	97
Sophie Selby (9)	98
Amy Terry (10)	99
Frankie Hadkiss (10)	100
Evie (8)	101
Halle Rose Cooper (10)	102
Oscar Spring (8)	103
Julianne Vu (10)	104
George Ash (8)	105
Alfie (10)	106
Caiden Gayle (9)	107
Mahad Hassan (8)	108
Louise Ridout (9)	109
Ayza Zahid (8)	110

Iqtidar Alam (7)	111
Isla Overill (10)	112
Riley Sculthorp (8)	113
Ben Robinson (7)	114
Chris Ryden (7)	115
Max D'Aiuto (9)	116
Liepa Briuchinaite (10)	117
Yağmur Hürriyetoğlu (7)	118
Kacie Levene (11)	119

St Thomas More RC Primary School, Birmingham

Adrianna Piszak (10)	120
Olivia Hussey (11)	121
Liliana Rak (8)	122
Faye Hogan (10)	123
Hanna Zawada (9)	124
Macy Lewis	125
Dorando Luis Mendoza (10)	126
Janice Cheuk Ka Ng (11)	127
Ava Stretton (8)	128
Gabriela Rak (11)	129
Luke Hussey (8)	130
Sonia Gorzelańczyk (8)	131
Millie Ward (10)	132
Teal Sutton (8)	133
Gracie Adams (9)	134
Macie-Leigh Moran Stokes (9)	135
Caitlan Fealy (10)	136
Sofia Brown (10)	137
Teya Vasileva (10)	138
Julia Kovalchuk (10)	139
Amelia Molloy (10)	140
Jaylen Hamilton (10)	141
Ella Ward (8)	142
Leah Crowley (10)	143
Millie Downing (8)	144
William Goodman (11)	145
Oliver Jones (10)	146
Fianna Nash (9)	147
Ethan Jones (8)	148
Ruby O'Neill (8)	149
William Wall	150

Sienna Boothe (8)	151
Esme Alara White (8)	152
Conor Joseph Flanagan (8)	153
Callum Hawkins (8)	154
Lawson Logan-McCann (10)	155
George Meade (10)	156
Joe Meade (8)	157
Jack Hulston (10)	158
Evangeline Mills (8)	159
Lillia-Jade Sandhu (8)	160
Ellis Gaughran (9)	161
Lexi Macleod (9)	162
Alana Crowley (10)	163
Julia Pierzchala (8)	164
Maximus Norton (9)	165
Fallon Logan-McCann (8)	166
Faith Bird (9)	167
Bobby Humphries (8)	168
Paris Maloney (9)	169
Luca Rughani (9)	170

Stoke Park Primary School, Lockleaze

Sienna Facciponti (8)	171
Sienna Hamblin (9)	172
Rowda Farah (10)	174
Poppie Quartley (9)	175

THE POEMS

Football Is The Best

F ootball is my favourite thing to do
O n Mondays and Thursdays I have football
O ff and on, I'm always playing football
T o be happy, you need to have fun
B all games are really fun for me
A ll my friends play football with me
L ots of my friends play football with me
L ots of times my papa plays football with me.

I love playing football with my friends
S ometimes I score a lot, I love it.

T he only time I don't play is when I rest
H appiness is good when I play football
E very time I play football it makes me happy.

B rilliant times of football is my dream
E very time I go to school I have to kick a ball
S ometimes I play FIFA not football
T o be good at football you need to practise.

Nathan Todd (9)
Annanhill Primary School, Kilmarnock

This Is Me!

Kaden.
Tall, dark blue eyes, brown hair, sporty and funny.
I am the son of Pauline and Steve, I am the brother of Callum, Dillon, Marcus and Ellie
Who loves their mum, dad, brothers and sister.
Who feels fabulous, jumpy and great.
Who finds happiness lying in bed, playing my Xbox and outside.
Who needs great friends, fresh air and good sleep.
Who gives help with taking in the shopping.
Who fears Covid, power cuts and storms.
Who would like to see no Covid, no pollution and no climate change.
Who enjoys staying up late at the weekend and having a midnight feast.
Who likes to wear under armour, warm clothes and warm gloves.
Be good instead of being rude, people will like you better.

Kaden Wright (9)
Annanhill Primary School, Kilmarnock

A Recipe To Make Me!

Ingredients you will need:
Ten teaspoons of fun,
Two cups of happiness,
Half a cup of hugs,
One jug of laughs
And finally a tiny teaspoon of anger.

First, grab an empty bowl, then pour the ten teaspoons of fun into the bowl.
After that, put the two cups of happiness in the bowl.
Next, take one jug of laughs and put it in a mixer.
After that, put in a tiny teaspoon of anger.
Once you have done that, mix it all together in the blender and put it in a tray, and put everything that's in the bowl in the tray.
Put the tray in the oven and wait thirty minutes.
After, leave it to cool down, and once it has, you have made me!

Ailsa Wightman (8)
Annanhill Primary School, Kilmarnock

Musical Me

I love music
I listen to music as loud as a roaring lion
When I hear music it makes me glow
But when I hear a rap I say no, no, no
When I look in the mirror I see a musician
Because music puts me in a good position
One Direction are my inspiration
And my motivation
I'm in a band like a rock star
When things are rough, they give me a hand
I play keyboard and a bit of guitar
If we make it big that would be bizarre
Now you know, I'm not what you see
Because this is me.

Beth Sommerville (9)
Annanhill Primary School, Kilmarnock

This Is Me!

Football is my boyhood dream
I'll shoot them all down like a laser beam
Chelsea legend Drogba
Has nothing compared to Pogba
I would rather be him than be a robber
Sadio Mane from Cameroon
Plays better in the afternoon
Haaland from Norway
Gets supersonic speed on the motorway
Jadon Sancho
Eats all the nachos
Messi from Argentina
Acts like a ballerina
Neymar from Brazil
Acts like a daffodil
Mohammed Salah from France
Can go to a dance.

Devyn Alexander (9)
Annanhill Primary School, Kilmarnock

This Is Me!

M y friends are Annelise, Caitlin and Jasmine.
I like gymnastics and dance.
L ike sushi, potatoes and sweets.
L ove my mum, dad, sister and my family.
I love my family friends.
E xcited and happy.

L ovely, kind, respectful and helpful.
I am happy and fabulous.
N ot mean and not ungrateful.
D oes not have ungrateful friends.
S assy and nice.
A mazing friend.
Y oung heart.

Millie Lindsay (9)
Annanhill Primary School, Kilmarnock

This Is Me

How to make Bronte Harper:

A teaspoon of art
Ninety-five grams of kindness
A dash of puppy love
Four teaspoons of happiness
Three pinches of height fears
Five grams of shyness.

First, add a teaspoon of art
Then add a dash of puppy love
After that, add ninety-five grams of kindness
Then just add three pinches of height fears
Now add five grams of shyness
And four teaspoons of happiness
Then leave in the oven for half an hour.

Bronte Harper (9)
Annanhill Primary School, Kilmarnock

The Tennis Girl

My name is Ruby
My favourite sport is tennis
I don't like when I miss the ball
When it bounces off the wall
One time I went to tennis
There were bouncy balls blowing everywhere
I love the game Jail or Bail
I like bailing my team
But I hate when the other team jails my team
I like when I hit over the net
Just like a jet
When I go against a girl called Evie
It's easy peasy
When I hit a serve
It feels like a tingly nerve.

Ruby Ferrara (9)
Annanhill Primary School, Kilmarnock

This Is Me

Add a sprinkle of nice.
After that, add 100 millilitres of kindness.
Then add 1000 millilitres of puppy love.
Then add thirty millilitres of dance.
After that, add a big spoonful of fun.
Five minutes later, add a mug of love.
Add a teaspoon of crazy.
Then add a medium cup of happiness.
After that, add a spoonful of kindness.
After all of that, add a mug of sporty.
This is me.

Jessica MacLean (9)
Annanhill Primary School, Kilmarnock

This Is The Recipe Of Me!

First, you need a splash of tallness.
Three tons of happiness.
Three splashes of funniness.
A jug of sportiness and competitiveness.
A tin of making a conversation fun.
Half an ocean of having amazing friends.
A box of cheesy Domino's pizza.
Half an ocean more of inspirational speaking parents.
A motto to go above and beyond!
This is how you make me,
So this is me!

Jack Speirs (9)
Annanhill Primary School, Kilmarnock

All About Me!

C aring when someone is hurt
A wesome at art
I ntelligent when I am at school
T all like a giant
L ong like a sausage dog
I nteresting when I am smart
N ice to all of my friends.

H ater of healthy food
A dog lover
T ank lover
T offee liker
I ce tea hater
E merald lover.

Caitlin Hattie (9)
Annanhill Primary School, Kilmarnock

This Is Daniel!

T he colour green is my favourite
H ugs from my mum and dad are my favourite
I like sleeping like a big bad bear
S ongs from the 80s and 90s are my favourites.

I love violin lessons
S oup made by my dad is my favourite.

M y brother annoys me a lot but I still love him
E ating noodles makes me really happy.

Daniel McGonigall (9)
Annanhill Primary School, Kilmarnock

Recipe

A pinch of clumsiness,
Lots of happiness,
Three pounds of madness,
Ten pounds of kindness,
Five teaspoons of smiles,
Five jars of hugs,
Lots of laziness,
Seven tons of craziness,
Four jugs of fidgeting,
Lots of love for Squishmallows,
Lots of hamster love,
Twenty pounds of confusion,
And *pow!*
You have made your own human!

Niamh Cunningham (9)
Annanhill Primary School, Kilmarnock

This Is Me

I'm tall
Green eyes
I'm a human
I have blonde and brownish hair
I have small ears
Big feet
Big legs
I'm funny
Short hair
Small hands
Can walk
Go to school
I'm very cool
I have black Adidas shoes
I have a purple shirt on
And have shorts with four pockets
What am I?

Answer: A boy.

Finley McPike (9)
Annanhill Primary School, Kilmarnock

This Is Me!

Sometimes I am mean.
I like make-up and I have green eyes.
I am the daughter of Chealsie and Conor and sister of Kaidy and Phoebe.
Lover of chocolate and my family.
Happy, angry, nice.
Play Roblox and Toca Boca.
Mum.
Can't sleep.
Thunder floods.
A week of school.
Dance and play outside.
Jasmine.
Be smart.
Moore.

Jasmine Moore (9)
Annanhill Primary School, Kilmarnock

This Is Me!

I am funny, cool, tall and I have blue eyes
I am son of Kelly and James and I am brother of Georgia
I am lover of Kelly and James and football and golf
I am happy, joyous and ecstatic
I have good friends and enjoy having fun
I give lots of hugs and lots of love
I enjoy playing golf and football and playing with my friends.

Lyle Anderson (9)
Annanhill Primary School, Kilmarnock

This Is Me! Music

When I started violin I thought I learned it like fire
Because it was dire
My mum said I was like The Incredibles
My favourite song is Wellerman
I might be in a band
I'm doing it like sand
Because I have a hand
Then I got the bow
And the toe
And I sow
I'm low as well
This is me.

Ben Havlin (9)
Annanhill Primary School, Kilmarnock

This Is Me

Small, blue eyes
Kind and generous
Son of Nicola and Paul
Brother of Finley, Emme and Dog
Happy, kind
I like playing with my pop its and phone
I give help with chores
I fear sharks and no sleep
Less Covid cases
Climbs trees like a monkey
I like to wear bright clothes
This is me.

Riley Reid (8)
Annanhill Primary School, Kilmarnock

The Riddle

I'm a human
I have blonde hair
I listen
I love animals
I wear hoodies
Nike shoes
Have lots of friends
I'm popular
I'm cool
My favourite animal is a panther
I hate tomatoes
I love sweets
What am I?

Answer: A boy.

Aric Alexander (9)
Annanhill Primary School, Kilmarnock

Baking

I love baking
It makes me so
Happy and all
I ever think is
Baking, I help
With dinner
All the time
Because I
Love to bake
If you know
Me all I want
To do is bake
It is so fun
To bake because
All I do is bake!

Ava Sword (8)
Annanhill Primary School, Kilmarnock

This Is Elspeth

I am a brave girl.
I have dark brown hair.
I am dyslexic.
I am crazy.
I hate tomatoes.
I love chicken noodle soup.
I like to spend time with my BFF.
I don't like to be alone.

Elspeth Clelland (9)
Annanhill Primary School, Kilmarnock

This Is Me

I have ears like a rabbit.
I have hands like spades.
I have blue eyes like the sea.
This is me!

I am as fast as a cheetah.
I am as happy as a smiley face.
I am as tall as a giraffe.
This is me!

I am as clumsy as a clown.
I have ginger hair.
I am as slim as a pencil.
This is me!

Carson Magee (7)
Antrim Primary School, Antrim

This Is Me!

I have hair like chocolate.
I have fingers like claws.
I have quietness like a mouse.
This is me!

I am as kind as an angel.
I am as happy as a sunny day.
I am as smart as an owl.
This is me!

I am as good as gold.
I am as fast as a raptor.
I am as fierce as a lion.
This is me!

Blake Lowe (7)
Antrim Primary School, Antrim

This Is Me

I have eyes like the sky
I have ears like a cat's
I have skin like peaches
This is me!

I am as fast as a volcano
I am as smart as an owl
I am as friendly as a cuddly bear
This is me!

I have hair like a brownie
I'm as good as an angel
I play like a dog
This is me!

Sofia Jennings-Patrick (8)
Antrim Primary School, Antrim

This Is Me!

I have eyes like the sea
I have cheeks like mushrooms
I have eyelashes like a cheetah
This is me!

I am as tall as a giraffe
I am as fast as a cheetah
I am as happy as a bunny
This is me!

I am as tall as a tree
I am as good as an angel
I am as fast as a dog
This is me!

Evie Murdough (7)
Antrim Primary School, Antrim

This Is Me

I have hair like chocolate
I have eyes like the sea
I have lips like strawberries
This is me.

I am as fast as a cheetah
I am as small as a snail
I am as mad as a volcano
This is me.

I have legs like a cheetah
I am really good at football
I am really smart
This is me.

Zack McManus (7)
Antrim Primary School, Antrim

This Is Me

I have eyes like chocolate.
This is me.
I have lips like pears.
This is me.
I have hair like chocolate.
This is me.

I am as smart as an owl.
This is me.
I am as quiet as a mouse.
This is me.
I am as brave as a bear.
This is me.
I am as good as a dog.
This is me.

Audrey Robinson-Bradbury (7)
Antrim Primary School, Antrim

This Is Me!

I have fists like metal
I have legs like springs
I have fingers like spikes
This is me!

I am as strong as a tornado
I am as dangerous as a whirlpool
I am as kind as a flower
This is me!

I am as good as gold
I am as strong as a rocket
I like adventures!
This is me!

Lucas Fox (7)
Antrim Primary School, Antrim

This Is Me!

I have eyes like grass.
I have ears like a cat.
I have feet like cheese.
This is me!

I am as clever as an owl.
I am as fast as a cheetah.
I am as good as an angel.
This is me!

I have hair like chocolate.
I am as good as God.
I have teeth like stones.
This is me!

Sienna Smyth (7)
Antrim Primary School, Antrim

This Is Me

I have eyes like the sea
I have hair like waves
I have hands like spades
This is me!

I am as angry as a bull
I am as big as an elephant
I am as flat as a pancake
This is me!

I am as silly as a chicken
I am as happy as a mouse
I am as small as an ant
This is me!

Harrison Shaw (7)
Antrim Primary School, Antrim

This Is Me

I have eyes like the sea.
I have hair like chocolate.
I have earrings like the stars.
This is me.

I am as fierce as a lion.
I am as good as gold.
I am as shy as a mouse.
This is me.

I am like a contortionist.
I love dogs.
I love going to the beach.
This is me.

Abbie Park (7)
Antrim Primary School, Antrim

This Is Me!

I have nails like claws
I have feet like carrots
I have muscles like rock
This is me!

I am as fast as a lion
I am as clever as an owl
I am as happy as a dolphin
This is me!

I am as tall as a tree
I am as friendly as a dolphin
I am as good as gold
This is me!

Jithendra Appapantula (7)
Antrim Primary School, Antrim

This Is Me!

I have eyes like chocolate
I have hands like jelly
I have a head like a ball
This is me!

I am as loud as a lion
I am as hungry as a panda
I am as clever as an owl
This is me!

I am as happy as a dog
I am as kind as God
I like playing videos
This is me!

Zixi Guo (7)
Antrim Primary School, Antrim

This Is Me!

I have eyes like diamonds
I have arms like pencils
I have legs like logs
This is me!

I am as hungry as a dog
I am as fast as a cat
I am as friendly as an elephant
This is me!

I am as smart as an owl
I am as tired as a koala
I like dogs
This is me!

Carter Rogers (8)
Antrim Primary School, Antrim

This Is Me!

I have eyes like grass
I have hair like chocolate
I have teeth like stones
This is me!

I am as funny as a clown
I am as quiet as a mouse
I am as kind as a teddy
This is me!

I am as smart as an owl
I am as nice as a dog
I love bunnies
This is me!

Ana Burrows (7)
Antrim Primary School, Antrim

This Is Me!

I am as funny as a clown
I have eyes like the sea
I have hair like the sun
I am as fast as a dog
This is me!

I have a nose like a strawberry
I am as fun as a puppy
I am as happy as a unicorn
I am as fierce as a lion
This is me!

Poppy Stewart (7)
Antrim Primary School, Antrim

Racing Roller Coasters

R acing roller coaster, zooming along the track
O utstanding speeds, full of fun and joy
L ooping, twisting, turning, and my dad screaming
L eaping on my seat, ready to rumble
E ating sandwiches in the queue
R eady to take off at any moment.

C hain lifts to get me to the top of the hill
O ld-fashioned roller coasters made of rotting wood
A lton Towers, my favourite park
S creaming loudly in fear when I reach the first drop
T aking in every moment, to remember it in years to come
E ager to go on the scariest rides
R unning back to the queue for a second go
S eatbelts securing me in place as the wind blows in my face.

Max Knight (8)
Horwich Parish CE Primary School, Horwich

The Countdown

Ten *long* minutes to go
Mum had told me, "Don't get up till eight."
My brain is exploding, I cannot wait
Toes are tingling
I hear sleigh bells jingling
7:52, eight minutes to go
Staring at the ceiling
The shivers that I am feeling
That are crawling up my back
I need to get my nerves on track
7:54, six minutes to go
Excitement runs through my veins
Imagining all the fun, imagining all the games
The Christmas dinner, there's so much, it piles
With all the love, it will make me run for miles
7:59, one minute to go
The family
Fifty seconds
The dinner
Forty-five seconds
The tree, the decorations

Thirty seconds
The aunties, the uncles, the grandparents
Nineteen seconds
The presents, the snow
Nine seconds
The coats, the scarves, the cold
Two seconds
The...

8:00.

Leah Stokes (10)
Horwich Parish CE Primary School, Horwich

I Like These

Poodles, noodles, I like these
Bing bang boo, the cat goes moo
Staring in the sky, looking at a fly
Hoola hoops and loop the loops, I like all of these
What's that lurking there, or was it just a bear
Apes and grapes, moles and poles
Seals, wheels, newts and flutes, I like all of these
Sunny summer days, trapped in a maze
Sophies, trophies, Taylors, sailors
Stellas, propellers, Myrtles, turtles, I like all of these
Twinkling stars, landing on Mars
Conkers, bonkers, clipperty clonkers
Pigs in wigs, leopards on shepherds, I like all of these
Owls on towels, puffins on muffins
These are things that represent me
I better be going, otherwise I'll miss my tea.

Freya Rushworth (9)
Horwich Parish CE Primary School, Horwich

The Next Step

The next step in life could be that
You could make a fancy hat.
Make it spin around your head
And then you don't touch it instead.
Make it go around all day
And when it stops, then you say,
"Make it dance, make it move,
Make it do a little groove."
Then make it sing the ascending scale,
Make it do it along a rail.
When it stops, then you make
A little bubblegum shake.
Teach the giraffes how to dance,
Teach the elephants how to prance.
Make chipmunks do the conga,
Then call them all Ponga.
These are all the things I want to do,
I just hope they all come true!

Stephanie McCarthy (11)
Horwich Parish CE Primary School, Horwich

Amelia's Poem

A mazing
M ighty
E nergetic
L oving
I ntelligent
A nd I'm cool.

I am Amelia, but I don't know where to start.
I love dogs, make-up and sparkly dresses.
My favourite food is Chinese, 'cause who doesn't love Chinese?

Amelia, Amelia, Amelia, Amelia, Amelia.

When I'm older, I want to be a vet
But everyone says I will have to work hard in school
And I don't like school.

Amelia, Amelia, Amelia, Amelia, Amelia!

Amelia Krinks (9)
Horwich Parish CE Primary School, Horwich

How To Make Maya

First, a cup of independence,
Then seventy grams of kindness,
And an ounce of curiosity.
This one is essential, if you want to make it sweet,
A love of drawing, now that's a lovely treat!
You must include ninety grams of that,
And writing stories too!
Two ounces of playing football,
And fifty grams of tall!
Now really, what makes me me,
The secret ingredient,
Is a love of animals!
Give it a mix,
Put it in the oven,
Then you should have Maya,
Who is really me.

Maya Ghosh (9)
Horwich Parish CE Primary School, Horwich

Football For Me

Football is inside me
It's who I want to be
It's called the beautiful game
And I love the thought of fame.

Football is inside me
It's who I want to be
The thought of the crowd
It will be so loud.

Football is inside me
It's who I want to be
Football is in my heart
When I run, I'm like a dart.

Football is me
It's who I will be
Being like my heroes
My hopes going up from zero.

Nathan Barrow (10)
Horwich Parish CE Primary School, Horwich

The Football Game

I wish, I dream,
To be good on my football team,
To play amazing as a striker,
To be like a tiger,
To tackle the person,
And run with the ball,
I could be tall,
I could be small,
I could be a hunter,
And shoot top corner,
Celebrating in front of the crowd,
With my team who are so proud,
After we win the game,
My coach says I burn like a flame,
I said I might never play the same,
This is why I like football games.

Lucas Trow (10)
Horwich Parish CE Primary School, Horwich

You Be You

I am taller than a giant, louder than a band.
All of a sudden, my friend takes me by the hand.
"I like you for you!" she said,
"And your long brown hair."
"I love me for me," she said,
"That's why we're best friends!"
"You're true, honest, independent, smart,
intelligent, silly and merrier than Mars!"
"A spoonful of kindness, a sprinkle of true, I am me, so you be you!"

Frankie Topham (11)
Horwich Parish CE Primary School, Horwich

Life Is Stupid

Life is stupid
When you fall down it laughs
And leaves you to struggle
You have to find your own way out
And once you have your freedom
You can live your life happily
You can make pancakes without fear
You can wake up without dread
You can live without terror
And you can get out of bed
Don't worry about life
It's nothing to be afraid of
Just dodge every bullet
And live it to the fullest.

Grayce Bulger (11)
Horwich Parish CE Primary School, Horwich

Who Am I?

I am a gymnast
I have dreams I want to accomplish
I have pets of many kinds
And a future waiting for me
Who am I?

I am a footballer
My dreams float by
I have a kind brother (don't count the arguments)
And a future waiting for me
Who am I?

I am a karate member
I have a guinea pig
Some doors have opened for me
My dreams and my future are here
Who am I?

I am me!

Isabella Leach (10)
Horwich Parish CE Primary School, Horwich

A Football Dream

The whistle blows as the players begin,
With roars from the crowd that take over,
As Ronaldo scores, oh what a player,
Then they defend like they are in the war,
Defending like they had no more,
Everyone has no more energy,
As Messi tries to score very intelligently,
As I celebrate after winning the game,
It is 3-0 once again,
I have a pint of beer and say hip hip hooray,
As I celebrate with passion.

Toby Zarins (10)
Horwich Parish CE Primary School, Horwich

How To Make A Jacob Walton

First, add a sprinkle of PlayStation to a glass bowl,
Second, thirty grams of nail biter,
Thirdly, 100 grams of McLaughlin powder,
Next, a tube of big brain liquid,
Then, one kilogram of sensible,
Sporty socks, full of smelly gas,
Stir 100,752 times clockwise, and three anticlockwise with a wooden spoon,
Lastly, add some small person powder with a pinch of loyalty.

This is a recipe for me.

Jacob Walton (10)
Horwich Parish CE Primary School, Horwich

Watch Out World Because This Is Me!

Watch our world because this is me,
I tend to be quite quirky,
Add funny to that,
I may be quite weird but that is just me.

I also like to be a loyal friend that might sometimes feel like jumping to Mars!
Sprinkle fuel because we're almost there,
I'm playful, jolly and love having fun, being myself is what I do
And so should you...

So watch out world because this is me.

Mbali Ndlovu (10)
Horwich Parish CE Primary School, Horwich

Things About Me

T houghtful is me.
H ome loving is me.
I ntelligent is me.
N ice is me.
G reat is me.
S weet is me.

A crafty person is me.
B ella is me.
O ut a lot is me.
U nbeatable at thumb war battles is me.
T iny but tall is me.

M yself is me.
E ating at lunchtime at school is me.

Isabella Benson (8)
Horwich Parish CE Primary School, Horwich

A Recipe For Me

A tablespoon of forgiveness.
Two grams of love.
A handful of positivity.
Two cups of helpfulness.
A spoon of kindness.
And two cups of sportiness.

Mix it all together until thick, soft and smooth.
Pour it into a big, red, heart-shaped tin.
Leave it in the oven for sixteen minutes.
Take it out, leave it to cool and give some to the whole wide world.

Alice Cheetham (7)
Horwich Parish CE Primary School, Horwich

I Dream

I dream, I dream
To play football for a team
I like to play striker
But sometimes I tire.

I dream, I dream
To be a farmer
Accompanied by a llama
Although it's impeccable
I'm sure it's acceptable.

I wonder, I wonder
Should I be a father
Would I rather
Boy or girl
Maybe neither.

Harrison Crossley (11)
Horwich Parish CE Primary School, Horwich

Recipe Poem For Me

A spoonful of kindness
A bowl full of laughter
A cup full of thoughtfulness
And a pan full of joy.

A quarter of a container of horses
Half a tin of animals
Two spoons of sports cones
And a glass of lemonade.

A plate full of music
A jar of gaming
Half a spoon of sleeping
And half a spoon of friends.

Tia-Raani Tuplin (9)
Horwich Parish CE Primary School, Horwich

Ella's Feeling Colours

Red, to show love and respect.
Yellow, to make it shine when you're feeling glum.
Green, to respect the nature all around you.
Blue, to cherish the fish in our ocean.
Pink, to show happiness with friends.
Orange, to feel bright even when it's night.
Black, to show the darkness we dislike.
Gold, to sparkle in our big world.

Ella Bolton (7)
Horwich Parish CE Primary School, Horwich

Colours Make A Change

Red to show my heart pumping, and love spreading out.
Blue to show the sky of kindness.
Pink to show roses who give out care.
Yellow to show the sun, shining with funniness.
Green to show nature, all around me.
White to show snow, full of playful children.
Gold to show award-winning people.
Black to show certain kinds of seeds.

Eloise Marland (7)
Horwich Parish CE Primary School, Horwich

This Is Me!

A sprinkle of football,
A dusting of friendship,
An ounce of loyalty,
What more could you want?

Fast runner,
Great passer,
Amazing scorer,
Could anything compare?

I dream of being a footballer,
Standing in the grounds,
Lights shining on me,
Cheering all around.

Ben Slater (10)
Horwich Parish CE Primary School, Horwich

A Recipe To Bake Me

A handful of kindness.
A tablespoon of love.
A sprinkle of caring.
Five grams of friendliness.
Two cups of forgiveness.
A teaspoon of helpfulness.
One drop of silliness.
Mix it all together until fluffy and soft.
Pour me in a tin.
Put in the oven and bake me.
Then I will be made.

Libby Fisher (7)
Horwich Parish CE Primary School, Horwich

This Is Me

T all as a skyscraper
H appy and helpful
I ndependent in work
S kilful when it comes to football.

I ntelligent in my maths
S haring is my nature.

M erry like everyone at Christmas
E nthusiastic like a monkey.

Jabe Cayton (11)
Horwich Parish CE Primary School, Horwich

A Recipe For Friends

A cup of kindness
Teaspoon of loyalty
Pinch of caution
Bowl of love
Half a spoon of respect
A handful of patience.

Put it in a bowl
Then blend it up with care
Put in a tub of truth
Put in the perfect pan
Then share with friends
And enjoy it.

Ernie Mollitt (9)
Horwich Parish CE Primary School, Horwich

This Is Me

Whatever you see is me
You will think I am normal
Well actually, this is me
I'm clumsy, intelligent, kind and friendly
Whenever you see me you will know it's me
So don't be afraid to write a poem
And laugh all you want
So get together and join in with me.

Jorgie-Leigh Burrows (9)
Horwich Parish CE Primary School, Horwich

Jessica

    J am sandwiches, mmm... delicious
    E ndless friendship
    S chool is where I made my friends
    S helter from the rain
    I support Manchester City Football Team
    C aring and kind
    A very annoying little sister...

This is me.

Jessica Hope (9)
Horwich Parish CE Primary School, Horwich

This Is Me

I really love the stars
The solar system and Mars
On my birthday, that was in June
I got a telescope to look at the moon.

My favourite animal is a cat
Although they would love to eat a rat
My favourite bird is a dove
All these things are the things I love.

Daniella Burns-Camus (10)
Horwich Parish CE Primary School, Horwich

Recipe For Me

A spoonful of fun,
A cup full of laughter,
Half a cup of kindness,
A bowl full of sports.

A quarter of thoughtful,
Two bowls of animals,
Two spoons of joy,
A pan full of play,
A glass full of movies.

This is all a mixture of me.

Kaitlin Chapman (9)
Horwich Parish CE Primary School, Horwich

A Recipe To Make Me

A handful of clumsiness.
Forty grams of sport.
Thirty grams of nature.
Thirty grams of speed.
Twelve grams of science.
A handful of animals.
Two grams of games.
Ninety grams of football
And then mix it all up together
And then you are done.

Stanley Birbeck (8)
Horwich Parish CE Primary School, Horwich

Be Yourself!

I'm a very kind person, and I care and I share
I'm a bit lazy, but not all of the time
I like a good run around, and once I found a 2p
I like to bake a big tasty cake! Yum!
I'm good with animals, especially my dog!

And that is me!

Niamh Wilkieson (9)
Horwich Parish CE Primary School, Horwich

What I Like!

J ogging is my favourite thing! I normally do it.
E nergetic as a giant lion!
F riendly as ever.
F irst to help!
R eady for anything!
E very school day is the best!
Y es, French is my favourite topic!

Jeffrey Smith (8)
Horwich Parish CE Primary School, Horwich

Skateboarding

I like skateboarding,
It's truly my thing
Going up and down ramps every time, saying, "Wee!"
Looking up to my hero, the name's Tony Hawk
Customising my deck with vibrant colours
Skating into the sunset
Skating with no fear.

Fern O'Brien (11)
Horwich Parish CE Primary School, Horwich

My Recipe That Makes Me

A handful of kindness.
A sprinkle of care.
A spoonful of funniness.
Two grams of love.
Stir together carefully until creamy and smooth.
Pour into love hearts and flowers of friendship.
Finally, share with everyone in the whole world.

Isabel Cheetham (7)
Horwich Parish CE Primary School, Horwich

This Is Me!

Eater, sleeper, daydreamer,
Walker, can be a talker,
Boring, snoring,
Likes to swim,
I'm very happy when I win,
The most important thing to me,
Is I love dogs,
But I also love my family,
Who always cares for me.

Amy Rose Grundy (9)
Horwich Parish CE Primary School, Horwich

Me!

E nergetic as a bee!
V ery weird when I want to be!
E xcited for adventure!
R eady to be ambitious!
L etter hater!
I love gymnastics!
E ver winning!

And that is me!

Everlie Williams-Hall (7)
Horwich Parish CE Primary School, Horwich

This Is Me
A kennings poem

McDonald's lover,
Nail picker,
Sport player,
Writer,
Animal lover,
Ingenius idea thinker,
Good listener,
A very good listener, actually,
Fruit lover,
Art maker,
This is me.

Leila Tucker (10)
Horwich Parish CE Primary School, Horwich

Rainbow

Red for love.
Orange for care and respect.
Yellow for sunshine and happy.
Green for freedom and friendship.
Blue for down and then get back up again.
Purple for friends and family.

Olivia Gagg (7)
Horwich Parish CE Primary School, Horwich

Rambo

I have a rabbit.
Not a tabbit, a rabbit.
My rabbit is black.
It wears a backpack.
I love my rabbit.

Layla Jackson (5)
Horwich Parish CE Primary School, Horwich

Pancake

I have a dog.
Not a pog, a dog.
My dog is white.
My dog is not bright.
I love my dog.

Daniel Tonu (5)
Horwich Parish CE Primary School, Horwich

Blue

I have a dog.
Not a log, a dog.
My dog is brown.
It wears a crown.
I love my dog.

Isabella Daley (6)
Horwich Parish CE Primary School, Horwich

Me!

Hi, my name is Olivia,
I prefer to be called Liv,
I also like to play trivia.
My favourite lesson is art,
Some of my family live near,
And some live apart.

I really love to skip,
And I really like lemons,
But with no pips.
My best friends are Zara and Ava,
I also love cake,
But with a lot of flavour.

My teacher is Miss Bliss,
I like to ask her questions,
Starting with Miss!
My eyes are very blue,
Don't ask me what 89x30 is,
Because I don't have a clue.

I love to bake,
Many different things,
But especially cake.
I am a lamb lover,
That's my favourite animal,
And I only have one brother.

I love Titanic,
I've watched it a lot,
And even now I still panic.
I'm in class 5BL,
I like English,
And not very good at spelling.

My favourite colour is brown,
I take care of a lot of people,
Even when they feel down.
I am ten,
I love farms,
But not the hens.

My birthday is 27th September,
I love to roller-skate,
The first time was in December.

I have a brother and a sister,
I love them so,
Even when my brother is a mister.

Olivia Gladden (10)
Scargill Junior School, Rainham

My Life

This is me, I like animals,
But my favourite is an elephant.
This is me, my life is a highway,
I have four siblings but I am a middle child.
I like drawing, this is all about me.

This is me, I like watching TV,
I hate strawberries, I like fidgets.
Also, I can calculate digits,
My biggest fears are spiders and bugs.

I have the body of steel and the heart of gold,
But wait until you unfold the fun in me.
I may not be the tallest,
I could possibly be the shortest.
I am straight and accurate, like a ruler
But beware there is more to fear.
I never stop I am like a train track always moving.

But goodbye, that's all for tonight,
Maybe one day I will be back,
I could be tall, I could be short,
I could be tall, come on, guess who I am.

Ayaat Salawe (11)
Scargill Junior School, Rainham

This Is Me

This is a person,
This is me.
The one who hates Roblox,
But loves Ari and Wengie.

This is a girl,
Who can do a fancy twirl.
The one who loves KitKat,
And someone who can chat.

Maya makes me laugh,
Fish fingers make me barf,
Cats remind me of giraffes,
So you see...

This is a person,
This is me,
The girl that's named Sade,
Can't you see?
I prefer Louise,
But call me Sade, it's fine.
I'm a pretty girl and really kind.
I'm truly someone that I care about.

Sweet and sour,
Has lots of power,
In love with emojicons.
Hello Kitty's my fave character.
Wish to be a singer.
Love a rose gold reindeer.
So you see.
This is a person.
This is me.

I'm unique and only one in 100,000 and three!

I have to go now,
We're going to do PE,
See you soon,
Remember me.

Sade Majoyeogbe (9)
Scargill Junior School, Rainham

This Is Me!

I am a mad movie watcher,
I am like a sleepy sloth when I watch them every day,
I am a professional baker,
I am the creator of cakes as sweet as heaven,
I am the best goalkeeper my friends have ever known
I am the best goalkeeper they will ever know.

I am a great friend, kind and friendly,
I will always be there for you,
I am nice, honest,
I am supportive and trustworthy,
I am prettier than a mad modeller,
I am the best at catwalking.

My hair is as brown as chocolate buttons,
My hair smells like chocolate pudding,
My freckles are as dotty as a ladybug's back, sweet and sensitive,
My freckles are like sprinkles on a delicious ice cream,

My eyes are brighter than the sky,
My eyes are like beautiful diamonds.

Libby Jobson (8)
Scargill Junior School, Rainham

This Is Me!

I am like a fish in the swimming pool,
I am a superstar swimmer when kicking my legs,
I am an amazing cook when cooking with my mum,
I am like Gordon Ramsay, skilful and talented,
I am as flexible as a noodle,
I am very good at doing round-offs.

I am a supportive friend, loyal and gentle,
I am a nice, happy person to be around,
I am always there when you are sad, and I will cheer you up,
I am a crazy clown, I make people laugh like monkeys,
I am a kind, caring person,
I am a curious, interesting person.

My hair is as curly as curly fries,
My eyes are as brown as a hazelnut,
My eyes are as big as chocolate buttons,
My hair is as big as my mum's plants,
My hands are as small as a rubber,
My eyelashes are very long.

Hannah Onaboye (8)
Scargill Junior School, Rainham

Things I Like

I am as curious as Einstein,
Who was once a very wise man,
I like thinking of card games strategies
And play them like cracking eggs in a pan

I like eating mouthfuls of algebra for breakfast
With the numbers walking right into my mouth.
The amount of anime I watch
Could be moulded into Big Ben, the bell.

I like hot-boiled rice and moist curries
That are as fresh as a winter's crisp;
The good life for me is the undiscovered planet of nature
With the leaves as the tree's hair.

I like reading the books of JK Rowling,
I am Harry Potter himself.
I like drawing with members of family,
I do it especially as it is a good deed.
The one thing that settles me most is a game of YuGiOh.

Tameem Wahhaj (10)
Scargill Junior School, Rainham

Create Me

Do you want to create me?
I'm a walking dictionary but quiet like a mouse.
If so, here are the ingredients:

Half a cup of curiosity
A pinch of creativity
A handful of kindness
One cup of animal loving
Three-quarters of a cup of intelligence
A pinch of laziness.

Method:
First, mix half a cup of curiosity and a handful of kindness together for approximately thirty seconds.
Next, pour in a pinch of creativity and a pinch of laziness and mix into the mixture you made previously, until the texture becomes dough-like.
Then, put it into the oven until it bubbles with fun.
After, pour the remaining ingredients on top like glazing doughnuts.

Lastly, let it cool down for ten minutes, then you're done.

Enjoy!

Hollie Morphew (10)
Scargill Junior School, Rainham

This Is Me

My name is Zara
My favourite animal's a dolphin
Everyone calls me Lara
I hate the smell of a bin
I don't like the name Barbra
I don't like the look of a car rim.

I would like to start a business in the future
I can do anything I want to
I really like my culture
I never like to go to the loo
I love to eat cake
I never know what to do.

My friends are Olivia and Ava
I love to play It
I love cookies when they have flavour
I don't really like to knit
I'm not a sailor
Sometimes I slip.

I love to play sports and paint
I never ever faint
I also like to bake and cook
I also love to read books.

Zara Kasule (9)
Scargill Junior School, Rainham

My Dog Betty

My dog Betty is the best pet you can own,
She takes only a few seconds to eat a bone.
She jumps as high as a traffic cone,
Kindness and happiness she has shown.

She is extremely cute,
And is like a TV on mute,
She runs as fast as Usain Bolt,
And surprisingly never moults.

She is as soft as the winter snow,
And we bought her not long ago.
She is now nearly three years old,
And she's as bright as gold.

Her favourite place is the park,
And she unexpectedly hates the dark.
She also barks quite a lot,
And in the summer her fur is hot.

Ana Maria Astefaniei (11)
Scargill Junior School, Rainham

Alphabetical

Add lots of colour like yellow and blue,
Add a piece broken from a chandelier,
After, wait for the dancing rainbows to appear!

Beware of the flood I made,
But I won't clean it up,
Because it keeps others entertained!

Crafts and chewing bubblegum,
Can also be the second name for fun,
Candy and soda is number one,
While catching a glimpse of my favourite movie,
Wish Dragon.

I am pieces from my favourite books,
Diary of a Wimpy Kid,
And I am glued to my favourite dish,
Pizza with cheese that stretches like slime.

Laiba Faheem (10)
Scargill Junior School, Rainham

All About My Dog, Brandy Fogg

I love my dog because it's named Brandy Fogg
I love that my dog plays with a frog
My dog eats fast like a man running in a cast
My dog drank out of the bog
My dog is cute like a mute
My dog is crazy like Mazie
My dog wears a hat that catches a bat
I love my dog that licks out of the bog
My dog loves to eat her meat
My dog's meat tasted like human feet
My dog is sometimes calm like a palm
My family loves my dog like a family log
My dog has snot like a robot
She has a snuffle mat that comes with a toy bat
This is my dog!

James Fogg (7)
Scargill Junior School, Rainham

How I Am!

I am a librarian, pretty but quiet,
I am a reading champion with super speed and passion,
I am a cookie dough, sweet and savoury,
I am as hungry as a lion, big but skinny,
I am a lover and I love my family like a pretty superstar.

I am funny like a comedy show but a bit more dramatic,
I am strong, big and fierce,
I am a peacock with nice clothes,
I am a Virgo, not ashamed to be.

My skin is as white as an albino monkey,
I am a brown-headed girl,
My eyes are a mix of green and brown,
This is me!

Lara Mahrous (9)
Scargill Junior School, Rainham

This Is Me!

C aring and kind as can be,
H ave me around and you will see.
L ovely to have as a friend,
O ther than that, I'll be with you till the end.
E verything you want is in me.

S omething you will see,
U nknown feelings emerge within me.
M e and you, forever,
M e and you, always together.
E verything's going to be okay till the end,
R eal struggles to find a friend.
S omething pops up, it's me, I will be your buddy, always.

Chloe Summers (10)
Scargill Junior School, Rainham

This Is Me

My favourite colour is red, I am from Pakistan
One place I don't want to go is Afghanistan
I may be funny but I can be friendly
I am amazing and my ruler is bendy.

I am smart but I am very chill
But I am a gamer so I need to wait at a till
My life is cool but I can't swim in a pool
I am very short so I need a stool.

I am very sporty and pretty nice
One thing I am scared of is a lot of mice
I am normally happy but sometimes sad
It's normally because of me being bad.

Syed Azeem (9)
Scargill Junior School, Rainham

This Is Me

T he most important thing in my life is dance!
H ard work is needed all of the time, I get very tired
I am nine years old, I am very independent
S ophie is my name and I am a summer baby.

I have a little sister who is so sweet to me
S he is very kind to me, she is as cute as a buzzing bee.

M y mum is the best, I remind myself every day
E very day in every way, I love her so much in every single way.

Sophie Selby (9)
Scargill Junior School, Rainham

Amy Terry Is...

A paintbrush at work
Cooler than Billie Eilish
A cheeky chimpanzee in class
Louder than a golden trumpet
Funnier than Alan Carr
An ant in the big blue ocean
As fast as a Tesla down a motorway
Tall like an emerald tree
As busy as a bee
More confusing than long division
As bright as a torch
As red as a tomato
Smarter than Stephen Hawking
Better baker than Paul Hollywood
A small balloon in history.

Amy Terry (10)
Scargill Junior School, Rainham

Frankie Hadkiss Is...

I'm a lightning bolt at maths
Leaping from calculation to calculation
A gymnast on parallel bars
Sporty like the Olympics
Curious trying new things
Exploring new places is what I do
I'm mini on the outside
But I've got a big personality on the inside
My face is filled with freckles
And my skin is light peach
My eyes are brighter than the sun
And sandy, light brown hair
This is me.

Frankie Hadkiss (10)
Scargill Junior School, Rainham

This Is Me!

I am an artist, creative,
And sometimes it goes wrong,
But always gets better.
I love my family
As much as red poppies.
I am sometimes sour,
But always sweet.
I am as shy as a snail,
I hardly speak or come out,
I am a dog,
Clumsy and furry.
My eyes are as blue
As the Pacific Ocean.
I am as small as a mouse,
My hair is as brunette as chocolate.

This is me!

Evie (8)
Scargill Junior School, Rainham

Halle Rose Is...

A famous traveller who travels the world.
A professional ice skater.
An explorer who finds a pot of gold at the end of the rainbow.
The first lady to go to Mars.
The only lady to own a spaceship in my back garden.
A superstar who walks the red carpet.

As kind as Mother's arms.
As sour as sweets.
Eyes as green as emeralds.
As small as a pencil.
As sneaky as a snake.

Halle Rose Cooper (10)
Scargill Junior School, Rainham

This Is Me

I am like a fish, fast at swimming,
I am like my family, nice and kind,
I am like an orange, sweet and good,
I am a scuba diver, strong and brave.

I am like a school councillor, kind and caring,
I am like a chicken, annoying and loud,
I am a picture, that falls every second.

My eyes are as green as grass,
I am as tall as a giraffe,
My hair is as blonde as the sand.

Oscar Spring (8)
Scargill Junior School, Rainham

A Demon Sat In The Dark

I go solo by myself,
I'm different to everybody else.
I'll slay if you don't obey,
Vengeance is my answer.

A laughing jester,
I like to break the rules.
Independent with a little help,
Lalisa is my idol.

I'll haunt you in my dreams and
I'll freak you while you're asleep.
A raging fire cutting everyone off,
I'm a demon.

Julianne Vu (10)
Scargill Junior School, Rainham

This Is Me!

I am a dolphin, big and brave,
I am as strong as a gorilla,
I am a shark, snappy and strong,
I am like a fish in a swimming pool.

I am as mad as a horse,
I am a sloth, slow and lazy,
I am a lion, energetic and brave,
I am as fast as a cheetah.

My hair is as blonde as a lion cub,
My eyes are as brown as dawn,
My hair is as bright as the beach.

George Ash (8)
Scargill Junior School, Rainham

All About Me!

Alfie is...
A cheetah at its fastest,
A pro master gamer,
An undiscovered planet,
As sneaky as Spider-Man,
As brave as Captain America,
As funny as the Joker,
As bored as a cloud,
As scary as Venom,
As tired as a sloth,
As tiny as an ant,
As cool as a spy,
As mysterious as a spy,
As lazy as a pillow,
As strong as the Hulk.

Alfie (10)
Scargill Junior School, Rainham

This Is Me

T he happy, proud uncle
H e loves to play football with his nephew
I s the sportiest one out of my family
S undays I hang out with my friends.

I 'm the smart one
S uspicious when my nephews go out.

M y nephews are important to me
E ducational at school.

Caiden Gayle (9)
Scargill Junior School, Rainham

Me And My Family

Taking care of my sisters
I love seeing the birds chirping
I really like playing
I love looking after people's pets
Yellow and blue are my favourite colours
I like football, I am as fast as a cheetah
I am as squeaky as a rabbit
Football is my thing
This is me.

Mahad Hassan (8)
Scargill Junior School, Rainham

This Is Me

L ovely and intelligent, that is me,
O verwhelming is what I choose to be,
U nique and funny is me every day,
I am a kid who likes to play,
S ports is what I like to do,
E xcept for tennis, that's one I don't like to go through.

Louise Ridout (9)
Scargill Junior School, Rainham

This Is Me

T houghtful
H elpful
I always help my family and friends
S uperhero comics are my favourite.

I love my family
S unday, I relax.

M r Bean is my favourite programme
E lephants are my favourite animal.

Ayza Zahid (8)
Scargill Junior School, Rainham

What Sport Am I?

You have to chop things in half with your hands.
As you get stronger, you have to punch harder things.
You need to fight people after training.
You have to be brave.
You can't give up or cry when you're fighting.
What sport am I?

Answer: Karate.

Iqtidar Alam (7)
Scargill Junior School, Rainham

This Is Me

T alented at art.
H elpful at home.
I ndependent in school.
S upportive for people.

I like summer!
S ometimes silly.

M ia Morris is my best friend.
E sio Trot is my favourite book.

Isla Overill (10)
Scargill Junior School, Rainham

All About Me!

T houghtful
H elpful
I always be silly at home
S illy Billy.

I love McDonald's
S unday is my match day.

M cDonald's is my favourite meal
E lephant ears are so big!

Riley Sculthorp (8)
Scargill Junior School, Rainham

I Am...

I am like Jordan Pickford
Early in the morning, energetic is me
When Mr Sun is out, I feel really happy
I am so fast
Just like a cheetah, I am
I am as springy as a frog
Sporty should be my first name
This is me.

Ben Robinson (7)
Scargill Junior School, Rainham

All About Me!

C reating is my favourite thing about art.
H ave you had a thing that was so important to you?
R eading is my favourite!
I love doing arts and crafts!
S hells are things that I love collecting.

Chris Ryden (7)
Scargill Junior School, Rainham

This Is Me

I am bouncing off the walls like a rabbit,
Talking as fast as a speeding bullet.
A smile is planted on my face,
I feel like I am having a sugar rush and I am as crazy as ever.
What am I?

Answer: Excited.

Max D'Aiuto (9)
Scargill Junior School, Rainham

Liepa Is...

An undiscovered continent,
A super, sneaky spy,
A tall standing tree,
Who wishes to be famous as could be,
A blue-eyed swimmer,
Hoping to be top of the league,
A quick cheetah,
And has a thing for PE.

Liepa Briuchinaite (10)
Scargill Junior School, Rainham

Girl That Likes Art

Creative like an artist,
I am like a sleepwalker in the morning,
When the bees start buzzing, the sun starts rising,
The butterflies start dancing in the sky in the morning,
It makes me feel happy like today.

Yağmur Hürriyetoğlu (7)
Scargill Junior School, Rainham

Kacie Levene Is...

Daisy soft
Sloth slow
The adventurous cat
In your neighbourhood
Teacher smart
Sweet ice cream
Craftier than an artist
Taller than the clouds
A sneaky spy
Funny dog.

Kacie Levene (11)
Scargill Junior School, Rainham

As I Fall Into A Dream

As I sit there, all alone,
My eyes droop down into sleep,
Everything is calming, every bone.
Like a symphony coming to a close, not a peep!
In the rhythmic rustling of the trees,
I enter the land of my dreams:
Graceful, gentle skaters, setting the scenes,
The phantasmagorical glimmer of a rising sun,
Proud, peaceful peacocks, prancing in the joy,
It's time to find some fun!
An opera full of mesmerising music, the perfect thing to enjoy,
A farm of guinea pigs, all to my pleasure!
Gallons of pumpkin soup, too much to measure!
All my friends, what a happy time we can spend together,
As the doorway gradually comes to a close,
I awake from my sleep, this is an adventure to remember!

Adrianna Piszak (10)
St Thomas More RC Primary School, Birmingham

The Ingredients That Make Me

There will only be one of me,
So I might as well live my life how I want it to be.
Two whole tablespoons of sport,
Footballs my dad bought,
Eating fish, I hate,
So with my parents I debate,
But I end up throwing it off my plate.
Every day I run a mile,
At the end I smile.
Football, cricket and tennis matches all day,
"You are a machine!" my family say.
For dinner, chicken curry,
It's so yummy.
A mini Gordan Ramsay I aspire to be,
I'll be cooking for the queen.
Also a runner is my dream,
This is why I'm so special and unique.
I'm truly me.

Olivia Hussey (11)
St Thomas More RC Primary School, Birmingham

I Am Happy, I Am Me

I am the colour white
So wonderfully bright
Bathing in the sunlight
Acting as a knight
Stealing all the spotlight
Of course it's alright.

I am winter
As cold as the heart of the Grinch
Which is a Christmas movie
You should go watch it.

I am England
So much to see about me
And my heart is filled with London
So much to do and see
Big Ben is my blood
Pumping around, no fleas!

But most importantly
I am happy I am me
I am unique and special
I like partying and I like tea.

Liliana Rak (8)
St Thomas More RC Primary School, Birmingham

Recipe For How I'm Made

I am the only one of me.
I am unique as can be.
I have a simple recipe.
That makes me, me.

A jug of happiness, every day for me.
A dollop of joy, for everyone.
A splash of positivity, everywhere I go.
A tub of music, or me to dance and sing.
A hint of creativity, in everything I do.
A hint of writing, to be joyful.
A drop of rudeness and impatience, because nobody is perfect.

That is my recipe for how you make me.
Because as I've said before, I am unique, I am happy being me.

Faye Hogan (10)
St Thomas More RC Primary School, Birmingham

This Is Me!

Hanna
Child of Lucas and Kate
Who is reliable and caring
Who loves reading and gaming
Who hates negative attitudes
Who wants to work at Dogs Trust
Who wishes to meet Billie Eilish
Who is scared of spiders and darkness
Who dreams of going to California and Paris
Who is determined to learn piano and recorder
Who values her family and friends
Who is proud of doctors, nurses and her cousin
Who believes in ghosts and evil spirits and histories
Who goes to St Thomas More School
Hanna.

Hanna Zawada (9)
St Thomas More RC Primary School, Birmingham

My Recipe Rhyme

First of all,
Let's start like this,
Grab a bowl,
Get a whisk,
Sprinkle classy and a pinch of sassy!
Curly hair from my very head...
Now get to bed!
Let's finish the rest from the very best, bake a cake.
Chocolate and sweets, a real treat.
Squash and juice, really nice,
And just for a fact, I like rice!
Ice cream with sprinkles and a cherry on top!
Add cherries (a lot).
If you made this recipe, you would obviously be messy,
And you would make a copy of me!

Macy Lewis
St Thomas More RC Primary School, Birmingham

This Is Me!

There is only one special me,
I live a life where I'm happy!
Sometimes scared or sad,
There is nobody like me.

A sprinkle of happiness, makes me smile,
A dash of exploring, I enjoy every mile,
Time with my family, I remember every moment,
A teaspoon of music, I hum every beat,
I go to different restaurants, I eat a lot of meat.

There is only one special me,
I live a life where I'm happy!
Sometimes scared or sad,
There is nobody like me.

Dorando Luis Mendoza (10)
St Thomas More RC Primary School, Birmingham

What Makes Me

Everyone is special as there will only be one of me.
But I will give you some tips to find yourself.
The recipe is easy, but it's what makes me.

A tablespoon of joyfulness, that can have fun.
Make yourself positive, don't be sad when somebody laughs at you.
Set a time to rest, it's always good for you.
Be happy, don't be worried, have fun with your families.

Everyone is special as there will only be one of me.
Follow these tips to find yourself.

Janice Cheuk Ka Ng (11)
St Thomas More RC Primary School, Birmingham

I Am Magical

I am pink
My cheeks are rosy
The colour of flowers in a bridal posy
I am blue
Like the sky on a summer day
Cloudy pictures drift away
I am spring
The dandelion and daisy
In the green grass
Lying down and being lazy
I am white
Like a fish in the light
I am everywhere
I am here and there
I am wise you see
I am eloquent and active
I am compassionate and kind.

I am me
I am special, you'll find.

Ava Stretton (8)
St Thomas More RC Primary School, Birmingham

Recipe For Friendship

Friendship is like a three-tier cake,
It can be hard to make,
But once it is ready it can be the best thing ever.

Here is a recipe to become friends:

A bag of kindness can go a long way,
A box of laughter can change the day,
A sprinkle of craziness makes life fun
And a pinch of welcoming makes me melt.

Friendship is like a three-tier cake,
It can be hard to make,
But once it is ready it can be the best thing ever.

Gabriela Rak (11)
St Thomas More RC Primary School, Birmingham

This Is Me!

I am red,
Poppies are red in their barley bed,
Fire is red,
And it will make you dead.

I am summer,
When it gets hotter and hotter,
There's no snow around,
That's not really a bother.

I am the park,
There's so much to see,
There are always conkers in autumn,
And not in other seasons.

I am me,
I am special and unique,
Like I'm at the beach,
What I hate is to cheat.

Luke Hussey (8)
St Thomas More RC Primary School, Birmingham

My Life In My Homeland

My homeland is Poland,
Don't want to leave.
When I needed to leave,
Obviously I wept.
Got family all around,
Not a space on the ground.
My family covered in yellow,
We love meadows.
Had to say goodbye to all of my friends,
Soon left my homeland.
Couple of days in the car,
Sister got no bars.
At my new home,
Where I cry a lot,
Because I miss Poland, my homeland.

Sonia Gorzelańczyk (8)
St Thomas More RC Primary School, Birmingham

All About Me!

There will always be one of me,
So special and unique.
A little recipe mixed up in me,
Following it doesn't take much,
It's absolutely free.

A daily mile, for a smile.
A sprinkle of friendliness, every time.
But there is always a teaspoon of sadness everywhere.

I will play cricket till the sun falls.
I will play with friends till the sun rises.
And that's me!

Millie Ward (10)
St Thomas More RC Primary School, Birmingham

All Of Teal's Year

I am blue,
Blue is the colour of a midnight sky
When it is passing by.
I am yellow,
Like the sun on a sunny day
When the clouds move out of the way.
I am winter,
When the snow comes down
And Santa comes to town.
I am autumn,
When the leaves fall on the ground.
I hear a falling sound.
I am keen like I have always been
But never mean like an angry bean.
I am me.

Teal Sutton (8)
St Thomas More RC Primary School, Birmingham

This Is Me!

G is for glasses, I pull off glasses quite smoothly.
R is for reliable, you can always rely on me.
A is for artistic, always willing to do a masterpiece.
C is for confident, I'm not afraid of anything.
I is for imaginative, I always have wild thoughts and ideas.
E is for energetic, I always have energy to do anything.

I am unique in my own way.

Gracie Adams (9)
St Thomas More RC Primary School, Birmingham

This Is Me, Macie!

M stands for magnificent and marvellous like my mom
A stands for artistic and amazing, always doing something creative
C stands for caring and considerate, looking after people when they're upset
I stands for inventive and intelligent, I love reading and making things
E stands for energetic and enthusiastic, I have lots of energy and I'm very enthusiastic.

Macie-Leigh Moran Stokes (9)
St Thomas More RC Primary School, Birmingham

What Makes Me, Me?

No one is like me,
A tablespoon of happiness,
A teaspoon of joy,
A fraction of sadness,
Playing outside all day until the night burns grey,
A pinch of turmeric for flavour like a Saturday night curry,
Matches of cricket and football all day,
Helping each other until it's time to go,
Say goodbye until tomorrow,
No one is like me because that's me being Me!

Caitlan Fealy (10)
St Thomas More RC Primary School, Birmingham

DIY Me!

There will be one of me, I can give some facts about me to reach my level of happiness that you may seek.

A spoonful of happiness, like a loving person,
A sprinkle of musical sound, playing in my ear,
A teaspoon of art like an objet d'art,
Another spoon of respectful, like somebody to trust.

There will be only one of me to reach my level of happiness that you may seek.

Sofia Brown (10)
St Thomas More RC Primary School, Birmingham

About Me

P ineapple is my favourite fruit.
U nicorns like rainbow animals are my favourite mythical creatures.
R ainbows I really like, they are a puff of colours in the sky.
P izzas are unhealthy but sometimes I eat them.
L emon yellow is my third favourite colour, blue is my second, purple is my first.
E nough things I have, my favourite is time with family.

Teya Vasileva (10)
St Thomas More RC Primary School, Birmingham

Me And You

A bucketful of care is all about me,
A happy sprinkle is full of me
And a pinch of craziness makes all of me.
But I'm a little different, and that makes all of me.
How to know me.
I'm a different person than you,
You know me more than I know you.
Now that I told you all of this
Now carry on and spread the word.
I told you, now you tell me.
Who are you?

Julia Kovalchuk (10)
St Thomas More RC Primary School, Birmingham

My Life In One Poem

A cup of tea to wake me up
With two teaspoons of sugar,
A dash of friendliness
And a dash of happiness.
For breakfast I eat waffles and butter.
Karate, I practice all day,
In a blink of an eye the day has gone by.
For dinner I have macaroni cheese
With carrots and peas.
This is me.
No one will ever be like me.
Everyone is different
And this is me.

Amelia Molloy (10)
St Thomas More RC Primary School, Birmingham

A Recipe About Me

What gets me out of bed is as wonderful as can be,
A cup of tea, two sugars, not three.
A drizzle of syrup and pancakes with heat
Is as beautiful as the sky in the night.
Football I play all day
Until the sky turns night and the stars fly.
For dinner I eat spaghetti and meat with melted cheese and mushy peas.
I run a mile for a smile then go to bed
Exhaustedly dead.

Jaylen Hamilton (10)
St Thomas More RC Primary School, Birmingham

My Life

I never give up with homework and helping
I am always up for a challenge
I like helping and playing with my sister and brother
My family makes me happy
My favourite colours are yellow, pink and purple
My BBFs are Ava, Harry and Layton and friends are Luke, Eris and Lilla
I help my family and friends with homework and dishes
And my BFF is Cheyne Rae, how did I forget.

Ella Ward (8)
St Thomas More RC Primary School, Birmingham

My Dream

P eace can bring
E veryone
A lways together to
C ommunicate.
E veryone can have
F un if you try to.
U sefulness can prove our
L ove but we have to learn how to.

W hether it's someone else
O r ourselves
R emember how to
L ove so we can
D ream of peace.

Leah Crowley (10)
St Thomas More RC Primary School, Birmingham

All About Me

Millie is my name
I am kind and caring
I like to spend time with my friends
Playing games and sharing.

On Saturday I go to dance
My favourite is freestyle
I do star jumps and high kicks
And the music makes me smile.

My family is important to me
I see them every day
We have lots of fun together
I love them in every way.

Millie Downing (8)
St Thomas More RC Primary School, Birmingham

What Makes Me, Me

There will only ever be one version of me, Will 0.1.
A bucketful of KFC makes me happy.
A very, very Happy Meal of twenty chicken nuggets and fries at McDonald's sends me to the skies.
A burping Burger King burger, double the fun and tastes yummy in a sesame seed bun.
The taste of Chinese chips brings me joy.
Roblox, alone or with friends, makes me smile.

William Goodman (11)
St Thomas More RC Primary School, Birmingham

There Is No One Like Me

There is no one like me
A sprinkle of sadness
A bucket of happiness
Hurting myself is what makes me not want to get up
But waking up to a good morning keeps me going.

Making and decorating my house with Halloween decorations makes me happy.
Playing outside with my friends till there's no daylight.
That's why there is no one like me.

Oliver Jones (10)
St Thomas More RC Primary School, Birmingham

This Is Me!

I am violet
Violet is the colour, violets and blossoms
A tint of blue, blue is the colour of my shoe
Violet, indigo, you don't know.

I am autumn
The season that makes you smile.

I am the conker
You may see
Round and brown
Light as can be.

I am me
I love to party
I love ice cream.

Fianna Nash (9)
St Thomas More RC Primary School, Birmingham

What I Need For Me On Sunday

Sunday morning,
Need to get out of bed
To get ready for a sunny day
For a Sunday match.
After Sunday match, get home
To have a bath
Then I go downstairs
To see my little brother
Go to get a PS4 controller to play FIFA 22
After my six-month-old brother had a bath
I went to play on my Switch
Until I had dinner.

Ethan Jones (8)
St Thomas More RC Primary School, Birmingham

This Is Me!

I am red,
Red for the poppies in the field.
I am yellow,
Yellow for the sunset.
I am autumn,
Autumn for the breeze.
I am spring,
Spring for the long grass.
I am a star,
A star shining among the crowd.
I am a circle,
A circle dancing and twirling around.
I am unique,
Uniquely friendly.
I am me.

Ruby O'Neill (8)
St Thomas More RC Primary School, Birmingham

This Is Me!

Ideas run through my brain,
The fun is done and the learning starts again,
School is where we learn,
Home is where we chill,
We eat and sleep and sometimes cheat,
At home we play,
At school we focus,
When we go home we eat,
Then we go once again and focus,
The next day is the weekend,
Now a big break from school.

William Wall
St Thomas More RC Primary School, Birmingham

All About Me!

All about me, yes please,
I love swimming in the sea.
Now that I am eight,
I love cake.
I am going to be nine
And have a dime.
I have family around,
The word seems like I am a lucky girl.
I went to the movies
And had some smoothies.
When I was eight I was great
And had to celebrate.
All about me!

Sienna Boothe (8)
St Thomas More RC Primary School, Birmingham

What Is Pink? What Is Winter?

What is pink?
Pink for the roses that bloom and blossom.

What is winter?
Flakes of snow drift away, children play and decorate.

I am New York, we say thanks to France for our present of romance.
I am the sun, when I shine faces gleam, but I do hope people redeem.
I am unique and that makes me myself.

Esme Alara White (8)
St Thomas More RC Primary School, Birmingham

What I Need For Me

Little lazy,
I'm so crazy,
This is scary,
I don't feel lairy,
I'm so quiet,
Only in class,
I love football,
Only on Sunday,
A little brave,
Definitely bossy,
Blaze through football players,
I never give up,
Only when I duel players,
This is it,
I'm so tired.

Conor Joseph Flanagan (8)
St Thomas More RC Primary School, Birmingham

Home Time

In school playing football.
It's really cool, it's a duel.
It's a draw?
I want to play more.
Working, chirping, finally it's home time.
The sun's shining like a chime.
Time to go now, I am going in my pool.
Hugo is gonna drool, he is a fool
But I love him.
Time to go to bed.

Callum Hawkins (8)
St Thomas More RC Primary School, Birmingham

This Is Me!

L oyal and lazy with a wicked smile.
A wesome and ambitious, here to be nutritious.
W onderful and wild, willing to go on an adventure.
S plendid and super, I'm a super trooper.
O riginal and open-minded, I'm the guy you need.
N oble and natural, as busy as I can be.

Lawson Logan-McCann (10)
St Thomas More RC Primary School, Birmingham

No One Is Like Me

I am different and unique
No one is like me
A bag of frightfulness
That is me
A spoon of sadness
That is me
A pinch of kindness
That is me
A fraction of funniness
That is me
A sprinkle of joy
That is me
I am different and unique
No one is like me.

George Meade (10)
St Thomas More RC Primary School, Birmingham

The Crazy Child

I am crazy because I run around
I be crazy
I go Koko every day.
Sometimes play but I am crazy
So I play crazy
Sometimes I can keep myself cool
But sometimes not
Sometimes fun
Sometimes not
I know I am crazy
But sometimes not
I am as brave as a crocodile.

Joe Meade (8)
St Thomas More RC Primary School, Birmingham

My Future

The future I want is,
Being as quiet as a ninja,
Being as quick as Usain Bolt,
Achieving my life goals,
Becoming famous worldwide,
Learning piano,
Making tech equipment,
To learn to make tools,
To be one of the first people to find a gem,
This is my future.

Jack Hulston (10)
St Thomas More RC Primary School, Birmingham

The Amazing Me

I am red
Smiley and bright
Red for the poppies and a red sunset
I am spring
The bright yellow daisy breaking through
I am playing
In the park
Searching for conkers
I am amazing
With many talents
I am special
I am kind to all
I am me.

Evangeline Mills (8)
St Thomas More RC Primary School, Birmingham

My Dreams

I'm kind and caring every day
I love my family and my friends
I wish I lived on a rainbow
I want a majestic, magnificent unicorn.

One day I will live on a cloud
I want a rainbow dog
I want a dog job
I love unicorns
I want to live on the sun.

Lillia-Jade Sandhu (8)
St Thomas More RC Primary School, Birmingham

I Am Me

I am blue
Blue like the colour of a noon summer sky
Watching the clouds pass by.
I am winter
As I skate on ice
I watch snowflakes fall by.
I am a lake
As canal boats sail by.
I am different
We're all not the same
This is what makes me!

Ellis Gaughran (9)
St Thomas More RC Primary School, Birmingham

This Is Me!

L   is for loyal and honest, always telling the truth.
E   is for elegant, always being graceful like a swan.
X   is for 'xcellent, always working hard and helping.
I   is for intelligent and imaginative, always thinking of new ways to explore.

Lexi Macleod (9)
St Thomas More RC Primary School, Birmingham

This Is Me!

Y ellow is my favourite colour
E xcited like my dog
L oves playing in the garden with my frog
L ike a ray of sun
O verall, always fun
W henever someone's got a frown, I'll be there to turn it around.

Alana Crowley (10)
St Thomas More RC Primary School, Birmingham

Yellow Mellow

Yellow!
I am yellow,
Like a sunflower in the meadow,
Growing high in the sky.
I stand where the summer sun shines,
Waiting for the rain to come.
In the summer flowers grow,
The smell of dandelions flows to me,
It makes me, me.

Julia Pierzchala (8)
St Thomas More RC Primary School, Birmingham

The Riddle Of Me

I am
Green
As green as grass
And I dance to brass.

I am
Spring
When blossoms bloom
And when animals show.

I am
Africa
The place where everything sighs
And where everything is used.

Maximus Norton (9)
St Thomas More RC Primary School, Birmingham

All About Me

F aithful and good at football
A dventurous
L oveable and loyal
L azy and lively
O pen and obviously fabulous in each and every way
N ormal and nice to everyone.

Fallon Logan-McCann (8)
St Thomas More RC Primary School, Birmingham

This Is Me

    F is for funny and kind
    A is for amusing and arty
    I is for interested in the life around me
    T is for truthful and always fair
    H is for honest and happy.

Faith Bird (9)
St Thomas More RC Primary School, Birmingham

Bobby The Brave

My name is Bobby the Brave
I never misbehave
My favourite thing is food
It puts me in a good mood
The best footballer is Jude
When I see him we shout, "Up the Blues!"

Bobby Humphries (8)
St Thomas More RC Primary School, Birmingham

This Is Me

P stands for precious!
A stands for artistic!
R stands for rare!
I stands for imaginative!
S stands for super!

Paris Maloney (9)
St Thomas More RC Primary School, Birmingham

This Is Me!

I am loyal and kind.
I wonder if violence will stop.
I can hear a lion's roar.
I see the distant planets.
I am loyal and kind.

Luca Rughani (9)
St Thomas More RC Primary School, Birmingham

Happiness

Happiness is looking at a sunset, pinky orange and beautiful.
Happiness is like tasting ice cream for dessert and spicy pizza.
Happiness is feeling kittens' or puppies' soft fur.
Happiness is listening to my favourite song
'A Million Dreams'.
Happiness is smelling the fresh air on a summer's day.
Happiness is playing with friends and seeing them smile.

Sienna Facciponti (8)
Stoke Park Primary School, Lockleaze

About Sienna

I am Sienna,
I love my dog and bunnies too,
I love all animals,
And I love going to the zoo.

I also love to dance,
I dance all the time,
Any kind of dance,
Street, tap or even line.

Street dance is my favourite,
I think it really rocks!
I do it in my bedroom,
I'm practicing TikToks.

Dancing makes me happy,
It's really helped me grow,
I can't wait for me and my sister
To do our show.

If you want to smile,
Get up and shake your bum,

You can even dance with your animals,
Or with your best chum.

Sienna Hamblin (9)
Stoke Park Primary School, Lockleaze

Me

Art, drama and drumming,
This is who I am.
Generosity, sharing and heart-warming,
This is who I am.
Athletic, board games and fashion,
This is who I am.
Self-love, independent and intelligent,
This is who I am.

Rowda Farah (10)
Stoke Park Primary School, Lockleaze

Rain

R ain is powerful, like a storm,
A nd also weak, like a flower
I n a storm, in the sun it's a rainbow.
N o rain today? See you tomorrow, rain!

Poppie Quartley (9)
Stoke Park Primary School, Lockleaze

YoungWriters Est. 1991

YOUNG WRITERS INFORMATION

We hope you have enjoyed reading this book – and that you will continue to in the coming years.

If you're the parent or family member of an enthusiastic poet or story writer, do visit our website www.youngwriters.co.uk/subscribe and sign up to receive news, competitions, writing challenges and tips, activities and much, much more! There's lots to keep budding writers motivated!

If you would like to order further copies of this book, or any of our other titles, then please give us a call or order via your online account.

Young Writers
Remus House
Coltsfoot Drive
Peterborough
PE2 9BF
(01733) 890066
info@youngwriters.co.uk

Join in the conversation!
Tips, news, giveaways and much more!

YoungWritersUK YoungWritersCW youngwriterscw